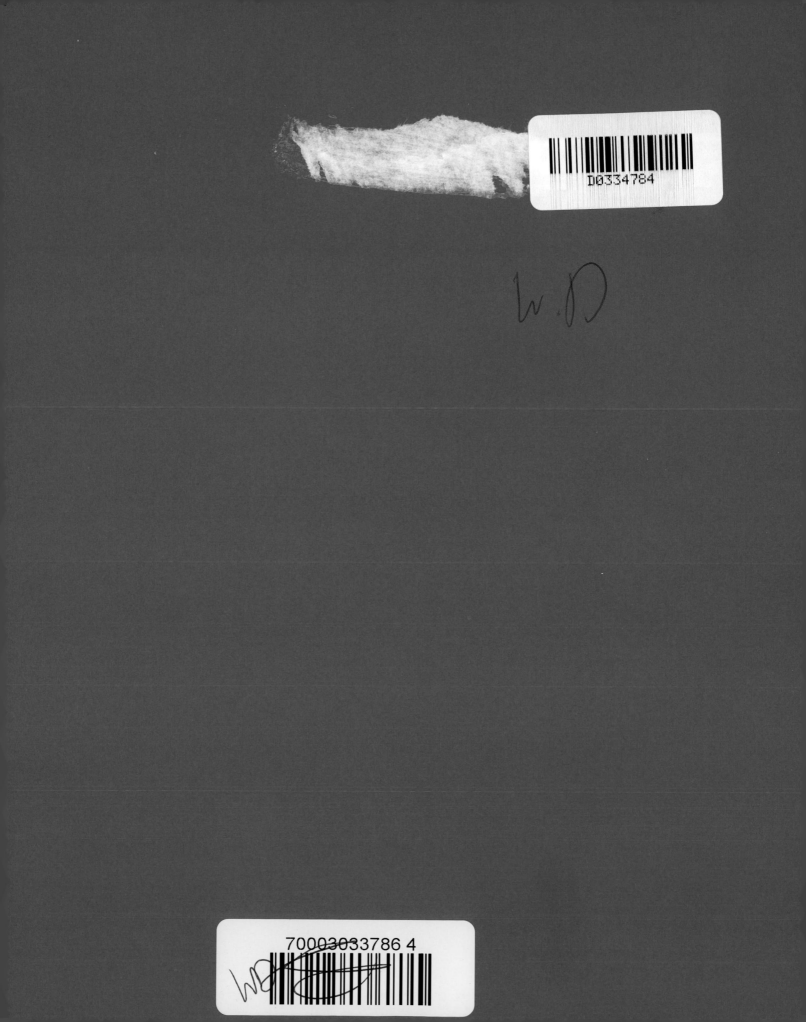

The Christmas Pine

Written by
Julia Donaldson

ALISON
GREEN
BOOKS

Illustrated by
Victoria Sandøy

Once upon a time I stood
With brothers and sisters in a wood.
The old trees told me I had grown
From a tiny seed inside a cone.

The whispering wind
was a friend of mine.
She said that I would
grow and shine.

I grew up tall.
I grew up high.

I grew until
I saw the sky.

Then came the day
they cut me down,

And carried me off
to a distant town.

I travelled far across the sea,

And now I am a Christmas tree.

Here I stand, in a city square.
I stand and shine in the winter air.

The lions keep
me company

And Nelson keeps
an eye on me,

And people pass
and stop awhile.
I love to see them
gaze and smile.

But more, yes, more than anything,

I love to hear the children sing.

Songs of reindeer,
songs of snow,
Reminding me
of long ago,

Songs of kings who travelled far,

And songs of light from a distant star.

I cannot stay
    forever here.
Another tree
    will come next year.

But think of me
    when I am gone;
Remember how
    I grew and shone.

And may the children
grow and shine,
Grow and shine
like the Christmas pine.

For Rob
J.D.

For my family
V.S.

The Christmas Pine is based on a true story. It celebrates a special tradition that stretches back over seventy years. Every year since 1947, the Mayor of Oslo in Norway presents the British people with a spectacular Christmas tree. The pine tree (usually a Norwegian spruce) is a symbol of peace and friendship: a thank you for the UK's support during World War II.

Norwegian foresters choose the tree months or even years ahead. They call it the Queen of the Forest and talk to it (and even hug it!) to make sure that the tree grows strong and tall. When the tree is fully grown, it's felled in a ceremony, before setting off on a long journey over sea and land.

It travels over a thousand kilometres – all the way to London's Trafalgar Square, where it stands proudly, shining with lights.

Each year, the UK Poetry Society asks a poet to write a poem to welcome the tree. Julia Donaldson originally wrote *The Christmas Pine* to celebrate the 2020 Christmas tree. The poem was performed by schoolchildren, and displayed in Trafalgar Square.

Back in Norway, the foresters are careful to plant more trees than they cut down, to make sure that their forests continue to grow. And they are always on the lookout for the next Queen of the Forest.

Published in the UK in 2021 by Alison Green Books, an imprint of Scholastic, Euston House, 24 Eversholt Street, London NW1 1DB
Scholastic Ireland, 89E Lagan Road, Dublin Industrial Estate, Glasnevin, Dublin D11 HP5F
www.scholastic.co.uk
Text © 2020 Julia Donaldson • Illustrations © 2021 Victoria Sandøy.
Moral rights asserted. *The Christmas Pine* poem was originally commissioned by The Poetry Society.
ISBN: 978 0 702310 16 4